Mr. Lawson walk
glared around at the class.

"A student in this room did something very dangerous last week," he began. He didn't even take off his overcoat first. "That student threw a mudball at my windshield while I was driving. Does that student want to come forward and admit what he did?" Mr. Lawson looked straight at me.

I looked down at my hands. "I didn't do it," I said in a low voice.

"Not only are you guilty, Mark, but by lying you're in double trouble." He let that sink in and then added, "I don't know where you learned this kind of behavior, but it certainly is unacceptable in my classroom."

"I didn't do it," I repeated.

"That's enough, young man. Perhaps you'll reconsider whether you did it or not while sitting out the baseball season."

If only this were a dream. A bad dream I could wake up from. But Mr. Lawson was really here. His face was red and angry. And I was really in trouble!

What's So Great About Fourth Grade?

Ellen Kahaner

Cover by Susan Tang
Illustrated by Paul Henry

Troll Associates

A TROLL BOOK, published by Troll Associates,
Mahwah, NJ 07430

10 9 8 7 6 5 4 3 2 1

What's So Great About Fourth Grade?

Thanks always to Leslie Freeman,
Gary Rothbart, Vicki Forman,
Mrs. McAndrews and her fourth-grade class,
and the Ragdale Foundation.

Chapter 1

I couldn't do division to save my life. How *did* you divide 20,000 by 20? The very first homework problem of the year, and I couldn't even figure out how it worked.

If only I could go outside. I made myself stop staring out the window. Come on, I told myself. Try. I put the 20,000 under the line. The divisor. It looked a lot like a baseball dugout. I put the 20 outside, like the pinch hitter who was never sure whether he'd be put in the game or not.

Now what? Come on, Mark Hunter. Try. But all I really wanted was to go outside and play ball. A little voice in my head said, "Add." I frowned. Add what? "Twenties." I added 20 and 20. Forty. I'd keep going until I got to 20,000. Then I'd count up how many twenties it took to get there.

I was on my sixty-third 20 when my father burst into my room. He was holding a floppy disk from his computer.

"Dad, I need help on this stuff . . ."

"Can't help now. My computer's crashed. The program's bombing! Have you seen my PC manual?"

I shook my head. "Maybe Deirdre's using it to prop up her dollhouse."

Deirdre was my seven-year-old sister. She could make anything disappear.

My dad looked over my shoulder at my homework. "I thought you did this stuff in third grade. Can't you figure this out yourself, Mark?"

"Well, it's just that I can't—"

"Sure you can! Just apply yourself!"

If I "applied" myself any more, I'd stick to the paper!

My father rushed into Deirdre's room. I heard things crash to the floor. He was tearing her room apart. Deirdre would probably tell my mother that *I* wrecked her room. My mother would shake her head. "Mark, have you been eating sugar again? You know it makes you hyper."

My mother was the nutritionist at our school

for ten hours a week. At home she was our nutritionist seven days a week, 24 hours a day.

I looked at the list of twenties on the paper in front of me. It was hopeless. I scrunched my homework and threw a perfect curve ball into the wastebasket.

The next morning at school I slid down in my seat so Mr. Lawson wouldn't notice me. Mr. Lawson was the toughest teacher at Southside Elementary. Everyone called him "The General" behind his back. His hair was gray and cut short and flat on top. He had mean-looking ears that stuck out from his head like satellite dishes.

I kept my eyes glued to my math homework. But I knew Mr. Lawson used radar. He'd somehow sense that I didn't know how to do the problem. If only the period would end before my turn.

I snuck a look at the board. To me the numbers were like a secret code that everyone else understood. My pencil slipped out of my sweaty hand. I bent down to pick it up.

Across the aisle Jerry was relacing his red hightops. Almost everything he owned was red. It was his lucky color. I coughed to get him to look at me. "I hate math!" I mouthed. I shook my head and rolled my eyes. Jerry nodded and grinned.

Then I looked at Scott, who sat in front of me. He had his math book propped open on his desk with his elbow. With his other hand he was trying to peel off a *Teenage Mutant Ninja Turtle* sticker that had gotten stuck on top of his desk. Scott collected stickers and toothpicks. Every time he ate a sandwich that came with a toothpick, he saved it.

Charles sat next to Scott, diagonally across from me. Charles was tapping his foot and nodding as if he were listening to music. He took electric guitar lessons after school. His hair was cut so short that we sometimes called him "Shine Head." He had on a black leather bracelet with silver studs on it.

"We do not play music in here, Charles," Mr. Lawson said out of nowhere.

Charles jumped. "I'm not."

"You're playing music in your mind, and that's the same thing."

Was thinking about something the same thing as doing it? I wrote down the question in my notebook. I'd worry about it later.

Mr. Lawson wrote the next problem on the board. "Who knows the answer?" he asked. Over near the corner Marcie the know-it-all waved her hand.

Mr. Lawson ignored her. "Eric?"

"I was just stretching," Eric said quickly.

Mr. Lawson picked up a math book. "You left this on my desk."

Eric turned red. He always forgot everything. Once last year he forgot to get dressed. He wore his pajamas and Garfield slippers to school!

Mr. Lawson put the book on Eric's desk.

"Thank you," Eric mumbled.

Mr. Lawson started walking up the aisle toward my desk. I gulped. Then, lucky for me, there was a knock on the classroom door.

"Must be the new student," Mr. Lawson said.

Everyone turned to look. I couldn't believe it. In walked Duncan Dover, the Albert Einstein of Southside Elementary. We'd known each other since kindergarten, and he lived on my block.

"This is Duncan Dover," Mr. Lawson said. "He's transferring into our class. Take the seat next to Mark." Duncan was a skinny kid with lots of freckles and a very thick pair of glasses. When you looked through the lenses of the glasses, the freckles looked gigantic.

I gave Duncan a big grin. It faded fast when Mr. Lawson said, "Mark, up to the board." My heart sank. But right when I stood up, the lunch bell rang. "Saved by the bell," I cheered, jumping out of my seat.

"All right, class. During tomorrow's math

period, we'll pick up where we left off." Mr. Lawson pointed at me.

My stomach turned. I looked over at Duncan. Help! I mouthed. Duncan grinned and gave me a quick signal. The tip of his index finger pressed to his thumb to make an O. The "okay" sign. I okayed him back. Maybe Duncan could get division through my thick skull.

Chapter 2

*L*ater that day I sat staring at the clock above the blackboard. The big hand was almost to the twelve, and the little hand was on the three. Baseball practice began a little after three P.M. Three P.M. was when real life began.

All the boys in the class showed up at practice. Even though team tryouts weren't until the spring, we practiced from September until the snow was so thick you had to wear boots instead of sneakers.

Finally the three P.M. bell rang. Minutes later all eighteen of us fourth graders were squashed together on the bench near home plate.

"Where's the General?" Jerry asked.

I saw Mr. Lawson crossing the field. "He's

our new coach?" I groaned. "He's still wearing a suit and tie! If his coaching is anything like his teaching, we'll probably get a quiz at the end of the game." Everyone laughed so hard the bench shook.

Mr. Lawson marched over and stood with his arms crossed over his chest. "Last year, you were zero for twenty," he said. "This year will be different. I'm your coach now, and I hate to lose."

There was a sudden hush among us. Mr. Lawson pointed to the outfield. "Warm up!" he commanded.

I looked at Jerry, Jerry looked at Eric, Eric looked at Scott, and Scott looked at Charles. Mr. Hartz, the music teacher, was our coach last year. He had us sing scales to warm up.

"Around the field, ten times!"

We got up slowly.

"Run, don't walk! What do you think this is, a turtle race?"

He sounded like a drill sergeant in the Marines. And that was just the beginning.

"Get out there on the field! Touch your toes. One, two! One, two! Circle your arms. I want speed! Now, shrug those shoulders and roll 'em!"

The torture went on until my muscles screamed. Just when I thought Mr. Lawson

17

had finished with us, he said, "Okay. Twenty sit-ups for good measure."

I was too tired to move. The whole team lay down flat on the field.

"What are you, wimps?"

We forced ourselves to do the sit-ups. Then we crawled back to the bench and collapsed.

"Come on, let's play ball!" Mr. Lawson was really excited now. His face was red and his eyes shone. "Charles, first in the batting order, Jerry, second, Scott, third, Eric, fourth. Mark, you're fifth." He sent the rest of the guys out on the field.

I sat on the edge of the bench and watched as Charles got on first, Jerry got a base hit, and Scott walked. Then Eric struck out, and Charles got tagged out trying to steal home.

"Two outs," Mr. Lawson called. "Hunter, you're up."

I gripped the bat. Nothing else mattered. Eye on the ball. Eye on the ball. I swung.

"Stt-rr-ike," Mr. Lawson yelled. "Take your time!"

I let the next pitch go.

"Ball one," Mr. Lawson said.

The ball came faster. I eyed it and swung.

"Swing and a miss!" Mr. Lawson shouted. "One ball, two strikes!"

"Come on, Mark!" Eric called from the dugout. "Put it away!"

I breathed deeply. I had to hit the ball. This time I watched and waited. Now! I swung. The ball cracked against the bat. It sailed up high and headed straight to Duncan Dover.

Duncan was standing as far right in right field as you could get. I ran to first. Duncan jumped for the ball. "I got it! I got it!" he yelled. The ball hit the ground hard and bounced away. Duncan had missed!

I practically walked around the bases. When I got to home plate, the guys slapped my back and cheered. By the end of the inning the score was 7 to 0. We switched sides.

I ran to my position at second base and got ready. I picked up a clump of dirt and rubbed it on my pants leg for luck. Lou Whitaker always did that before a game, and he was one of the best. I looked around. Jerry was tightening the red scarf around his neck and winding up his pitching arm. Scott did a deep knee bend behind the plate. He stopped to pick up something in the dirt. He grinned and held a twig up for me to see.

"For your collection?" I called out.

"A prehistoric toothpick!" he yelled. He put the twig in his pocket.

Eric looked as if he were conducting an orchestra at first base. I knew he was just getting loose.

"Yo, Shine Head!" I called to Charles at

third. He waved. The studs on his bracelet glinted in the sun. We were ready. Jerry struck out two guys in a row. Then Duncan stepped up to the plate. Jerry wound up and pitched. Duncan swung and spun around.

"Strike one!" Mr. Lawson yelled.

Duncan took off his glasses and wiped them with his shirt. Then he put them back on and squinted at Jerry.

Jerry threw a nice'n easy pitch.

Duncan swung the bat as if he were hitting someone over the head.

"Strike two!" Mr. Lawson yelled.

Jerry wound up slowly and then threw a steady, straight pitch.

Duncan swung hard and let go of the bat.

"Hit the decks!" Mr. Lawson shouted.

Everyone crouched down. The bat flew through the air and landed with a thud on the third base line. Duncan's mouth dropped open. No one said anything. The inning was over.

When the game broke up, I went over to Duncan. "Where are you going?" I asked him. He shrugged, red-faced.

"Come on, we're going in the same direction." I tossed my baseball from my hand to my glove. Duncan frowned.

We started walking. "It's the game that's eating you, right?" I said.

He nodded. His hands were clenched into fists.

"It's no big deal," I said to calm him down. "Anybody can have a bad day. I think it's your timing."

"Maybe," Duncan admitted. "Chess is really my game."

"I could show you a few tricks at baseball."

"I'll never hit that ball," Duncan sighed.

"If you can teach me long division, I can teach you anything," I insisted.

He looked at me. "How?" he asked.

"Uh, practice!" I said. "Practice always works. Plus, I'll keep all my fingers crossed."

"And your toes," Duncan said with a grin.

"So it's a deal?"

Duncan thought it over. Then he said, "I'll call you tonight about the math."

We slapped hands. Fourth grade was looking better already.

◆ Chapter 3 ◆

I sat in the dining room chair closest to the phone in the hallway. I didn't want to miss Duncan's call.

"Pass the butter," Deirdre said.

"You can reach it yourself."

"Mark!" my father said.

"It isn't butter. It's polyunsaturated margarine," my mother said.

"Pass the *polyunsaturated margarine,* dopuss," Deirdre said.

"No 'dopuss' at dinner!" My father looked at my mother. "What's a dopuss?"

"A dope and a sourpuss," I said. "That's the kind of joke second graders come up with all the time."

"Do not," Deirdre said.

"Do so," I said.

"Okay, okay," my mother said. She tapped her water glass with her fork. "Enough arguing. I have an announcement." She looked around with an important expression.

"So? Make your announcement." My father waited. He held a dinner roll halfway to his mouth.

Mom put her fork down. "I've decided to quit my job."

Even Deirdre was quiet for a moment. My father frowned and cleared his throat. "What do you mean? Why?"

"I'm going to start a catering business," my mother said proudly.

"What's a catering business?" Deirdre asked.

"I'm going to cook special food for parties and meetings," my mother explained. "People pay a lot of money for that."

"Who will make our lunches and dinners . . . let alone clean up?" my father asked. There was a sharp edge to his voice.

"Don't rush me. That's part of the announcement," my mother said cheerfully. "Mark, help me clear the table."

My father followed her with his eyes. He looked suspicious. I picked up some dishes and followed Mom into the kitchen. I watched her take a folder from the cupboard above the sink. She gave me a big smile as we went back into the dining room together.

"Ta-da!" she said, beaming. "Plan A!" She unfolded a computer printout on the dining room table.

"You used my computer," my father said.

"I had to."

"Was it still working when you finished?" He took a big bite of the roll.

"I didn't break your darling machine, Al." My mother swept the crumbs off the printout.

"Here's Plan A," my mother continued. "I've divided the household tasks. Al, you're to make dinner forty percent of the time. I'll take care of the other sixty percent. Mark, you have ten percent of the cleaning responsibilities."

I looked at the chart. Next to my name it said, "Vacuum living room," and under that, "Mop kitchen floor." Then there was a line like a branch on a tree, and it pointed to the words: "Pick up Deirdre after school and on weekends."

My stomach dropped to the floor. I looked for Deirdre's name on the chart. All it said next to her name was "Make bed" and "Pick up clothes."

"How come Deirdre only has to make her bed and pick up her clothes?" I asked.

"Deirdre's just in second grade," my mother explained.

My father stared at the chart. "Where's the money coming from to start this new business?"

"We'll talk about that later. You'll see. It's a great plan. It won't take nearly as much of your free time as you think." She smiled at my father. "And if it works out, *I'll* be able to pay at least half of our living expenses."

"You will?" My father looked interested. He put the rest of his roll down. "I don't like it. I'll try it, but I do not like it." My mother kissed him on the cheek. Had they both gone crazy?

"What about *my* free time?" I exploded.

My father frowned. "Calm down," he said. "You'll still have plenty of time for homework *after* dinner."

"I'm not talking about homework. What about baseball practice?"

"Not that again." My father groaned. "If you spent more time on your homework and didn't waste so much time throwing a baseball around, maybe you'd get a decent report card once in a while!"

"Great!" I said. "Just great!" I stomped up to my room and slammed my door so hard it popped back open. Baseball was not a waste of time! It was the only thing I loved.

I went to the door and listened. "Let him alone. He'll do okay in school," my mother was saying.

"I want him to do better than okay," my father said.

I looked around for my baseball glove. Holding it helped me think. Where had I put it?

I tossed my pillow to the floor and pulled the blankets off my bed. Nowhere. I looked under my desk and behind my bookcase. Maybe it was in my closet. I threw my clothes around and slammed the door. I opened my dresser drawers, picked through my shirts, socks, and underwear. Nothing.

I looked at the poster of Babe Ruth that hung over my bed. "If you were me, where would you look?" I asked the poster. "Of course, the doorknob!" I answered. I turned around and saw Deirdre walking past my doorway. Her baby doll was wrapped in a little pink blanket cradled in my baseball glove!

"Thief!" I shouted, and jumped up. "Give me my glove!"

"Leave me alone," she said. "It's past my bedtime." She rushed into her room and slammed the door. I went in after her and stood there, glaring at her. I wanted to wrap a bat around her neck. "Give me my glove," I said in my scariest voice.

Deirdre's eyes got as wide as quarters. "Take it," she said. "It's too hard for my baby, anyway."

She threw the glove at me and I caught it. I

27

made a monster face at her until she screamed and dove under her covers. Then I went back to my room.

"Mark called me a thief," I heard Deirdre say in the hall a minute later.

"He what?" Before I could defend myself, my mother appeared in the doorway to my room. She gasped at the mess.

"This is not good, Mark. Start Plan A right away!" She taped a copy of Plan A on the wall between my pennant banners.

"But Mom, if Deirdre hadn't taken my glove—"

"I mean now! No ifs, ands, or buts!" She marched out of my room.

I stuck out my tongue at Plan A. Then I checked to make sure the coast was clear. It was. I tiptoed out to the hall, picked up the phone, and dialed Duncan's number. I stretched the cord to my room and closed the door.

"I was just going to call *you*," he said.

"What a nightmare! My mom's starting her own business all of a sudden and expects us to cook and clean. She calls it Plan A! It's bad enough that I have a brat for a sister who takes my things without asking. Now I have to baby-sit her every afternoon and on weekends. That kills my baseball time!"

"Definitely the pits."

"I know." I took a deep breath.

"Did you finish the math problems?"

"Sort of," I said. "But I know they're all wrong. I can't figure out division, and I never will." I socked my pillow hard.

"Mark, you have baseball cards, right?"

"Sure, why?"

"Get one."

I shrugged and reached over to the table next to my bed. I had a whole album.

"Okay, so?"

"Take one out."

I picked out the awesome first baseman. "It's Mattingly," I said.

"Look at the back," Duncan said. "What's his batting average?"

I read the back of the card. "At bat 450 times last season with 150 hits."

"Okay. Listen. Take the number of times at bat and divide that into the number of hits."

"What?"

"If you divide 150 by 450, it's one-third, and you put it in the hundreds. His average is a .333."

"Oh, I get it, .333 is the batting average." I jumped up and heard the phone fall to the floor in the hallway.

"Hello?" I asked, running out to the hall and picking up the phone.

"No problem. It's only my ears you're destroying, Hunter." Duncan laughed. "Okay.

There are 25 players on a team and 350 players in the league. How many teams are there?"

I pictured the teams in the American League east and west.

"You divide 350 by 25," he said. "It's 14."

"Fourteen." I paced back and forth across my room.

Duncan turned the rest of our homework problems into baseball problems. When we finished, I wound up my right arm and pitched an imaginary curve ball to Babe Ruth. My whole body was tingling.

"Hey, Dunc, I'm going to show you a few tricks before practice tomorrow, okay?"

Duncan groaned, but he sounded happy. "Remember—fingers crossed," he said.

"And toes."

I ran downstairs to grab something to eat and found my parents in the den.

"Mark," my father said. "Look, I'm sorry I lost my temper at the table. But we're going to stick to last year's rule. If you keep up your grades, you can play all the ball you want."

"Sure, Dad, that's fine."

Mom looked surprised. "Mark, your father is serious."

"Okay, okay." I went into the kitchen. My mother followed me in, opened the refrigerator door, and took out her latest dessert creation. She called it "airplane cake." The top layer was cut in two halves and stuck in the bottom layer standing up in a V shape.

"Like wings," she explained when my father came in and raised his eyebrows.

"I'll take a sample flight." My father stuffed a piece of cake into his mouth. He started to cough. I handed him a glass of water. He took a few sips.

"Well?" asked my mother. "What do you think?"

"I think your business may turn out to be good for this family after all," Dad said. He turned away from Mom and grinned at me.

Chapter 4

*T*he next day after school the other kids waited for me at the baseball field. I was late because of Deirdre. I ran over, dragging her behind me.

"Don't pull," she whined.

"Chill out," I snapped back.

"Move it, Mark!" Jerry called.

"I have to take the brat to ballet," I said, out of breath. "I'll be right back."

Deirdre glared at me. "How come you're not wearing your apron, Mark?" she teased, darting out of reach. "Where's your mop?"

The other boys grinned.

"What's going on, dude?" Charles asked.

"That's enough, jerk." I grabbed Deirdre's arm. "Let's go."

"Jerk! That stands for Junior Educated Rich Kid," Deirdre said over her shoulder to the guys. I dragged her away before she could embarrass me anymore.

Saturday morning I woke up from a great dream. I was in a big stadium, and I'd just hit a homer. The ball flew up, up and away over the fence into a pile of dry, crunchy leaves in old man Hadler's backyard.

I lay in bed and stared at the bumps on the ceiling. I remembered Plan A and wished I could go back to the dream.

It wasn't fair that I had to clean the house. It wasn't! And to make things worse, I'd let all the housework pile up until today. On Tuesday, when I was supposed to vacuum the living room rug, I had decided to wait until Wednesday. On Wednesday I was supposed to vacuum the living room and mop the kitchen floor, but I figured it could wait till Thursday. On Thursday it was so close to the weekend, I thought it made more sense to wait until Saturday and do a really thorough job.

I threw my pillow across the room hard and knocked over my trash can. If I cleaned up fast, I told myself, I still might make it to practice on time. I got dressed quickly and went to the living room. I moved the vacuum back and forth on the living room rug.

Were you supposed to leave the carpet shag standing up or smooth it down? Standing up, it looked like I had vacuumed. Smoothed down, the rug looked shiny and worn like it always did. I left it standing.

Then the vacuum started making weird, choking noises. It coughed up some dust. I looked at the side of the machine. "Bag full" blinked back at me. That was it. I couldn't vacuum anymore. I unplugged the vacuum, hooked the cord on top, and dragged it back to the closet.

I remembered how the vacuum cleaner used to scare me when I was little. It made so much noise, and it looked like a humongous bug crawling across the floor.

Looking over my shoulder, I saw that the vacuum had left a thin trail of dust between its wheels. Gross! I stuffed the machine into the closet and rubbed the dust into the carpet with my sneakers. Then I rushed into the kitchen to get the mop.

I found the note on the kitchen table. It said, "Hi, Mark. The vacuum cleaner bags are under the sink. Please change the bag before you start vacuuming. It's easy! Just follow the directions. Thanks, honey! Love, Mom."

I imagined writing a note of my own to "Polly's Pointers" at the *Herald Eagle*.

Dear Polly,

I'm new to the cleaning game. How do you change a vacuum cleaner bag so you don't make a dust storm in the middle of your living room?

Sincerely,
Mark Hunter

By the time I started mopping the kitchen floor, I saw on the clock that it was lunchtime. Practice had started two hours ago! I squeezed some dishwashing soap into the big metal bucket, turned on the faucets full force, and aimed the hose into the bucket. I squirted myself in the eyes a few times, and got my shirt soaking wet. But I didn't care. I was in a hurry. Give me baseball or give me death!

The bucket weighed a ton, and when I put it on the floor, the water splashed over the edge like a tidal wave. The mop was the stringy kind, so I pretended I was Popeye, swaying back and forth on the kitchen floor. I made a big muscle with my arm.

Suddenly my feet started to slide out from under me. I looked down. There was plenty of water all over the floor, but it was sudsy water, and the more I scrubbed, the sudsier it got. Why wasn't the floor getting cleaner? The water was a grayish color. From my sneakers? Were you supposed to wash the floor barefoot? A wave of water traveled from one side of the kitchen to the other with every swab of the mop.

Dear Polly,
I never thought I'd be writing to you again so soon, but could you please tell me how to clean up after a flood, and how to prevent future floods?

Sinking fast,
Mark Hunter

I decided to let it air-dry. I raced out of the house and all the way to the baseball field. My sneakers made squishing sounds with each step. By the time I joined the game it was the bottom half of the *ninth* inning! But at least I was out of the house and not cleaning. I waved to the guys and said "hi" to Mr. Lawson.

"Glad you finally made it, Hunter. Why don't you go up to bat?" Mr. Lawson said. It was Jerry's turn. I looked over at him, but he waved me on. I grabbed the bat and ran over to home plate. I took a few practice swings, leaned forward, and waited. The ball came toward me fast. I didn't hear a single sound except the crack of my bat against the ball, deep and hollow.

"Awesome!"

"Excellent!"

"Wow!"

I ran faster, faster around the bases. From far away I heard the guys whistle and cheer. I slid easily into home. It was the easiest homer I'd ever run. Jerry gave me the high five, and I felt the slaps on my back and shoulders from the other guys.

Mr. Lawson nodded thoughtfully, studying me. "With Hunter heading our lineup, we have a chance at winning after all," he said at last. A big grin spread over my face, and I didn't care who saw it.

The other guys started breaking up to go home. Duncan took his time coming in from the outfield.

"Hey, Dover, let's practice!" I yelled. I was in a good mood from practice, and I really wanted to play.

But Duncan looked as if he were going to be sick. "Do I have to?" he said.

"C'mon. You'll like it!"

Duncan grumbled some more, but his lips twisted up a little when I handed him the bat.

"Grip the bat with both hands together," I told him.

Duncan pushed his glasses up on his nose. Then he folded his hands around the bat.

"No. Not like that. Line up the knuckles of one hand with the other." He did it. "Okay. Swing level and follow it through."

I made him do it over and over till he got it right. Then I showed him how to hold the ball. "Grip with two fingers on one seam and the thumb on the other. That gives the ball spin."

Duncan tried it. "My hand aches!"

"You'll get used to it," I answered. "With practice."

Duncan nodded. He looked like he felt a little better. "I gotta get home for dinner," he said. He picked up his sweat shirt from the bench and pulled it on over his head. "Aren't you supposed to pick up Deirdre from Brownies today?"

I stopped dead and stared at him. Oh no! How could I have forgotten? I swallowed. I was two hours late. My father would kill me. Suppose something happened to her? I took a deep breath. She'd be okay.

"Someone must've taken her home by now," I said. Duncan raised his eyebrows, but he didn't say anything. We started walking—fast—toward home.

It isn't fair, I told myself as we practically ran down the street. I can't be responsible for everything. I stopped to pull off my sweat shirt and tie it around my waist. I felt sweaty all over. Sweaty and creepy.

Then I imagined Mr. Lawson's voice: "You're as good a player as Rich Abel, Mark," it said to me. I repeated the sentence to myself. I liked the sound of the words. Imagine being a high school all-star like Rich was. I could just hear the voice over the loudspeaker at the game. Two simple words bringing the crowd to its feet as I ran onto the field. "Mark Hunter!" I ran up the steps to my front door. From the sidewalk, Duncan called good-bye.

As I opened the door, I heard my father yell, "Mark?"

"Yeah, Dad?" I said. He came into the living room. He was wearing an apron and quilted oven mitts on his hands. He held an eggbeater in one hand, and a spatula in the other.

"Hi, Mom!" I said. "Have a nice day?"

Then I saw the storm on his face. "Where have you been?" he said. "Can't you even remember to pick up your own sister?"

"I'm sorry," I stammered. "I just forgot! I hit a home run at baseball practice, and Mr. Lawson said I was good enough to—"

Just then Deirdre skipped into the living room. She held up two fingers of her right hand, the Brownie greeting, and smirked. I tried to grab her, but she jumped away.

"Be prepared," she said. "That's the Brownie motto."

My father wasn't finished with me. "What about your math test? It's Monday, isn't it? You're supposed to do your schoolwork before you play ball." He waved the spatula in the air.

I sniffed the air. "What's that smell?" I asked.

"The hot dogs!" my father yelled. We raced to the stove.

He pulled open the broiler an inch at a time. A small flame was burning in the pan. As we were staring at it, the smoke alarm on the ceiling went off. My father pulled the hose from the sink and aimed it full force at the fire, the stove, and the whole kitchen. Another flood. That was two in one day, so far.

"Call the fire department!" Deirdre shouted over the screech of the alarm.

My father ignored her. "How do you turn the alarm off?"

"Unplug it?" I offered.

He frowned. "Stand back. Don't do anything. Especially don't call the fire department." He disappeared down to the basement and came back with a stool. He put the stool under the fire alarm. Then he climbed up on it and took out the batteries.

Suddenly the screeching stopped. My father climbed down from the stool. "Done!" he said loudly. He bent down to the broiler and stabbed at the burnt hot dog with a fork. It crumbled into ashes.

"It's okay," I said. "I like 'em well done."

"We could make s'mores for dessert," Deirdre suggested.

I wasn't in the mood for a Brownie special, especially one where everything melted together.

My father shook his head. "No way. Kids, we're eating fast food tonight whether your mother likes it or not!"

Chapter 5

*L*ast year, Ms. Maxwell was my teacher and school was fun. Ms. Maxwell showed us how to make Thanksgiving turkeys out of cupcake papers. She hung them on strings from the ceiling. There was also a bulletin board called "Incredible Indians." We tacked up the headdresses we made. When we were really good, Ms. Maxwell put an extra feather on our headdress. Ten feathers meant you got a gold badge on your headdress. Then you were a chief. I was a chief.

On rainy days like today, Ms. Maxwell would hang a poster of a kid with a yellow raincoat and boots on the blackboard. She'd write on the board: "I've never seen slicker work," and then she'd return our homework with a smile.

But the only decoration in Mr. Lawson's classroom was the "Not Alloweds" list on the blackboard, which grew longer every day. I wanted to put a copy of that list in my scrapbook, so that in 25 years, when I described the worst year of my life to my own kids, they'd understand. This afternoon Mr. Lawson was about to add to his list again.

Charles had been whispering a song to Marcie.

"Do you want to sing for all of us, Charles?" Mr. Lawson had asked.

Charles shook his head.

"How about you, Ms. Jackson?"

"No," she said, blushing.

Mr. Lawson turned his back and wrote item number 58 on his list: "No whispered singing!"

Then Mr. Lawson wrote our math homework assignment on the board. He took a long time writing it.

When he stepped out of the way there were loud gasps.

He'd assigned almost 50 long division problems! On top of all our other homework! Ms. Maxwell had never given homework on holiday weekends.

I was still copying down the homework when the bell rang. If it took this long to write the assignment down, imagine how long it would take to do it! Everybody else would be taking second helpings of turkey and stuffing while I slaved away over my math homework.

I met Duncan outside the door.

"It's only November, and Mr. Lawson's 'Not Alloweds' list has taken over our lives," Duncan grumbled.

"And on top of that," I said, "it had to go and rain."

We walked to the baseball field, taking turns kicking a rock as hard as we could along the sidewalk until it landed with a splash in a puddle by the dugout.

I looked at the field. It was drowned in an inch of water. There was no way we'd get to practice. "First we get a ton of homework, now a ton of mud," I said. "Today is my lucky day." We started to walk home.

"Hey!" Duncan said. "How about the overpass?" He pointed to the narrow stone bridge that crossed over the highway near where we lived.

"What about it?"

"We can go up there and watch the cars go by down below," Duncan said.

"Yeah. Remember the time we tried to make that truck driver blow his horn?"

"He blew it so hard we almost fell off the bridge," Duncan laughed.

We climbed up the stone steps, leaned over the railing, and looked down. The cars were zipping by really fast, sending waves of water up with their tires. We decided to count the number of red sedans. When we got bored with that, we waved at the drivers to see how many would wave back. Then no car went by for a while. We watched and waited.

"I know what we can do!" I said finally. "Come on!"

I started down the steps. Duncan hesitated, pushing his glasses up on his nose. "Hunter, I don't like that look in your eye," he said.

But he followed me anyway. In the ditch beside the road I bent down and picked up a handful of mud. I formed it into a ball in my hand. I set the ball on the ground and grabbed some more mud.

"Help me," I said to Duncan, starting on my second mudball.

"What are you up to?" Duncan asked doubtfully.

"We're going to practice pitching," I said. "It's okay. Nobody'll get hurt." I looked at the row of mudballs and picked one up. I eyed a round gray stone on the other side of the highway, raised my arm, and threw. My mudball splotched against the rock.

"Your turn," I said to Duncan. Out of the corner of my eye I saw a bright red jacket. It was Jerry. "Yo, dude!" I called. Jerry waved and walked over.

"Pitch it to the rock," I said to Duncan.

Duncan picked up a mudball and bent his arm back.

"Sink it in there! Now!"

Duncan threw.

"Nice!" I said as the mudball sailed up high.

"Good pitch," Jerry said.

A dark blue coupe came speeding along the highway. The next sound we heard was a loud thump.

"Uh-oh," Duncan said. The blue car pulled to the side of the road and screeched to a halt. We froze. A car door slammed. I looked at Duncan. His eyes were wide. Jerry gasped and took off, running.

I turned to watch the driver cross the highway toward us. Cars honked as he waited on the median for traffic to clear. As he got nearer, I realized who the driver was. I'd recognize that short gray hair anywhere. Mr. Lawson!

"Run!" I yelled, pulling Duncan's arm.

We started running up the road.

"Stop!" Mr. Lawson called after us. "You'll be sorry!" The traffic on the highway cleared and Mr. Lawson crossed the road.

I ran ahead of Duncan. My feet felt light and heavy at the same time. It was weird.

"This way, Dunc." I pointed to an alley between two rows of houses with garbage cans every few feet. I knew this alley. I'd played

hide-and-seek in it for years. There was a secret door all the way at the end. If we just made it to there, we could duck through and escape.

"Run, Duncan!" I yelled, seeing Mr. Lawson looming closer and Duncan falling farther behind. I wasn't going to make it to the secret door. I looked around.

There was a garbage can with its lid hanging off. It was empty. I climbed in and closed the lid. Yuk! It smelled and was damp and dark inside. My heart beat a mile a minute. I could hardly breathe. After a few seconds I peered out over the edge.

I looked just in time to see Mr. Lawson grab Duncan by the shoulders. "Duncan Dover!" Mr. Lawson said.

Duncan grabbed his glasses before they fell completely off.

Mr. Lawson jammed his finger into Duncan's face. "Did you throw that mudball at my car?"

"No, sir, M-M-Mark did it!" Duncan said.

I felt as if I'd been socked in the stomach. Duncan was accusing me! His best friend!

Mr. Lawson nodded. "That figures. Mark never had any trouble hitting a moving target!" Then he shook his head. "He cracked the windshield of my new Dodge! You tell him for me, I'm going to call his parents tonight. We'll just see about this!" He let go of Duncan and marched off.

I climbed out of the garbage can. Duncan stood still.

"Sorry, Mark. I didn't mean it," he said. He looked as if he were going to cry.

I looked him in the eye. "Didn't mean it!" I spat out. "Tell that to Mr. Lawson, not to me!" I pushed him in the shoulder and started walking home as fast as I could.

Duncan followed me. "Please, Mark. I'm sorry."

"So am I," I said, feeling my throat burn. I felt like punching him. How could he? I started to run, and I kept running all the way home.

The minute I opened the door I smelled burnt bacon. Good. Maybe my father wouldn't see me or smell me. I ran upstairs and jumped into the shower.

"Dinner, dopuss," Deirdre shouted through the door.

"Dopuss yourself," I said.

I sat at one end of the dinner table, and Deirdre sat at the other. My father sat in the middle and passed a tray of sandwiches. Deirdre took one. I could hear her chewing the crunchy bacon. I ate a few bites of the toast and stared at my plate. The phone rang.

"I'll get it," my father said. My stomach

clenched. I waited. My father came back to the table, frowning.

"Mr. Lawson said you were throwing mud-balls onto the highway," he said. "And you hit his car. How could you do something so stupid, Mark? It's going to cost six hundred dollars to replace Mr. Lawson's windshield."

"I didn't do it."

"Do what?" Deirdre said.

"You're going to have to wash and wax Mr. Lawson's car on the next nice day."

"Duncan did it," I said.

"Did *what*?" Deirdre said.

"You expect me to believe Duncan could throw a mudball hard enough to break a windshield?" My father ignored Deirdre and frowned at me.

I could see I wasn't going to convince him. So I got up from the table and went up to my room. I ripped Plan A off the wall. Why wouldn't he believe me? My own father.

A moment later the phone rang again. I knew who it was this time and I didn't want to talk to him. I picked up the receiver. Then I put it back down before Duncan could say anything.

I didn't talk to him all weekend.

Monday morning it felt as if there were lead weights on my feet. I walked to school in slow motion. What was Mr. Lawson going to do now? What if he yelled at me in front of everyone? If only I could make myself invisible.

I got to my seat just before the bell rang. Duncan was staring out the window. He didn't even look at me. Then Mr. Lawson walked into the room and glared around at the class.

"A student in this room did something very dangerous last week," he began. He didn't even take off his overcoat first. "That student threw a mudball at my windshield while I was driving. Does that student want to come forward and admit what he did?" Mr. Lawson looked straight at me.

I looked down at my hands. "I didn't do it," I said in a low voice.

"Not only are you guilty, Mark, but by lying you're in double trouble." He let that sink in and then added, "I don't know where you learned this kind of behavior, but it certainly is unacceptable in my classroom."

"I didn't do it," I repeated.

"That's enough, young man. Perhaps you'll reconsider whether you did it or not while sitting out the baseball season."

If only this were a dream. A bad dream I could wake up from. But Mr. Lawson was really here. His face was red and angry. And I was really in trouble!

I watched Duncan go up to Mr. Lawson's

desk. He bent down and whispered something to Mr. Lawson.

Maybe he was telling him the truth—that he'd thrown the mudball, not me. But as Duncan straightened up he didn't turn and look at me. He didn't mouth the words "I'm sorry." He took the wooden hall pass from the corner of Mr. Lawson's desk, pulled open the door of the classroom, and marched out.

I felt anger burn in my throat. How dumb I was! I'd trusted Duncan and he'd turned on me. My stomach twisted into a tight ball. He'd pay for this. He'd pay.

Chapter 6

*A*t lunch I didn't sit next to Duncan. Duncan sat by himself in a corner of the lunchroom. I looked around. Jerry and Scott waved me over to their table. Eric and Charles joined us there.

"Duncan threw that mudball," Jerry told the guys. "I saw him." His cheeks were as red as his shirt.

"Duncan's a liar," Eric said.

Scott agreed. "Too bad about the team," he said to me.

"Maybe the General will change his mind," Charles said. "Without you the team is nothing." He shook his head. "He's a grade-A jerk."

"Who, Duncan or the General?" Jerry asked.

"Both," Charles said, laughing.

I looked over at Duncan. He was hunched over his looseleaf notebook. Didn't he ever stop studying? I spilled my lunch out from my bag onto the tray. Just wait, Duncan, I told myself. I opened a tiny foil package. Inside was a skinny little cucumber sandwich in the shape of a triangle. I laughed and opened another package.

"Anybody want to guess what my mother catered last night?" I held up a round sandwich with pink filling. The guys laughed loudly.

"My dog's Christmas party?" Jerry said. Everyone laughed.

"I know, an English tea. My mother was talking about it this morning," Eric said.

Eric was right, but I felt the ball of anger again. "Nope. It was Duncan Dover's birthday party. And we've got all these leftovers because nobody went." I said it loud enough for Duncan to hear.

But Duncan just ignored me and that made me madder.

"Watch this," I said to the other guys. I stood up and carried my tray over to where Duncan was sitting. I dumped my tray out onto Duncan's table. Jerry and Scott followed with their trays and dumped them out on the table too. Then Charles and Eric did the same thing.

"You're a dirty liar," Jerry said to Duncan.

Duncan turned red. I was glad. He *was* a dirty liar. Then Jerry threw his arm around my shoulder. "The team's going to be boring from now on," he said to me. "You want to toss a ball around sometime? Just us, without any squealers around?"

"Sure," I said loudly. I looked at Duncan, but he pretended not to notice. "I'll play ball with you anytime, Jerry."

Fractions. I sat at my desk at home and wrote the word in fancy script across the top of the blank piece of paper that was supposed to be my math homework. FRACTIONS! I wrote the word again with an exclamation mark after it and drew a bubble around it like in a comic book. Then I crumpled the paper and threw it over my shoulder. I read the problem out loud:

"If the post office is seven-eighths of a mile from school and the gas station is three-quarters of a mile from school, how much farther from school is the post office than the gas station?"

Maybe I would understand it if I wrote the problem out. The problem now stared back at me in my own handwriting. I still didn't have a clue about how to do it. I could ask my father, but he'd probably get mad. He didn't like to answer questions while he was working.

I called up Jerry. He wasn't much better in

math than me. I could hear a football game on TV in the background. I called Eric next, but his mother said he was taking a bath. Charles said he had no idea how the problem worked, and anyway, he was busy tuning his guitar. So I called Scott.

"I got an answer, but I don't know how," he said. "It just came to me."

"Well, what is it?" I asked.

"One and a half."

I shrugged and wrote 1 1/2 on my blank sheet of paper. I gave up. Math was beyond dumb. It was dorky.

The next morning we were standing around the schoolyard in a circle, waiting for the bell to ring.

"How about math?" Jerry asked me. "Did you ever get the answers?"

"Nope." I felt helpless about math. I looked over at Duncan. How could someone who was a filthy liar have it so easy with math? It wasn't fair. "I bet I know someone who did." I nodded at Duncan. His face was bright red from the cold. He held his notebook tightly against his skinny chest. I walked over to him. I looked over my shoulder back at the guys and gave them a big grin. Then I grabbed Duncan's notebook, pulled off my gloves, and started leafing through his math section.

"Give it back!" Duncan said, trying to grab the notebook back. I ignored him and kept looking for his homework. Finally I saw the neat handwriting, the columns of numbers, and the carefully corrected mistakes. I pulled the whole page out of Duncan's book.

"Check this out!" I passed Duncan's homework around to the other guys. After they'd had a good look, I stuffed the crumpled sheet of paper back into Duncan's notebook and handed it to him. Duncan walked away, fast. From the back I could see his ears burning bright red.

"Thanks, Mark!" Jerry slapped me on the back. The final bell rang and everyone went into the building.

"After I collect the homework," Mr. Lawson told us, "you may read quietly while I go over your work."

All the guys fidgeted nervously while Mr. Lawson paged through the stack of homework papers. Finally he put the papers down, looked up, and said, "I must say I'm very pleased with how well you all did with fractions. So instead of using the rest of the period to go over the homework, we'll move right along." He handed some papers to Jerry.

"Pass these out," Mr. Lawson said.

"Oh, no," Jerry whispered.

"What is it?" I asked.

"A quiz. This should be easy for you," Mr. Lawson said.

"Oh, now we've had it," Charles whispered. I caught a few nasty looks from the other kids and then looked down at the problems. It was hopeless. I stared at them, hoping to break the code. I couldn't. Nothing happened. Five minutes later Duncan walked up the aisle and turned his paper in. I looked back at my blank paper.

"Pencils down!" Mr. Lawson said, clapping his hands.

I felt a terrible sinking sensation in my stomach. I'd never figure out this number junk. Maybe I really had something wrong with me. Maybe I was really dumb. And to top it off, I couldn't even do the one thing I was great at! I'd gotten kicked off baseball for something that wasn't even my fault! Talk about being a fourth-grade loser!

Chapter 7

"Who knows how to spell the word for a person who copies another person's homework and passes it off as his own?" Mr. Lawson asked the next morning, starting the spelling lesson.

No one around me volunteered. M-a-r-k, I thought.

"I'll give you a hint. The word starts with a C and ends with a T." Mr. Lawson walked up the aisle. "Jerry?"

Jerry tapped a red pencil on his notebook. I hoped Jerry wouldn't tell on me. I held my breath. He shook his head.

"Scott, would you like to guess?"

"No, sir."

"Eric?"

Eric screwed up his face. "I forgot."

"All right. Since I can assume the rest of you 'forgot,' I'll remind you." Mr. Lawson wrote on the blackboard C-H-E-A-T, and underlined it three times. "Because no one admits to cheating on the math homework"—he stroked his chin and thought it over—"I think it fitting and fair to punish the whole class. There are seven days left until Christmas. Double homework assignments until then. Anyone have a problem with that?"

A few groans escaped. Mr. Lawson raised an eyebrow. "One other thing . . ." He straightened the papers on his desk and then looked up. "Rumor has it that there have been food fights in the cafeteria lately. Any truth to that, Mr. Hunter?"

This caught me off guard. "I wouldn't call them food fights," I said finally. "They're more like food *throws*." I expected the guys to laugh. No one did.

"I find back talk very amusing. Maybe you'll find it funny to sit in the classroom during lunch from now on so you can entertain *me*."

Mr. Lawson snapped open the window shades. The bright December sun made me blink hard. I hoped no one saw how red my face was. Everybody threw food around in the cafeteria. Even Mr. Warner, who served the

63

soup, threw sponges at the kids. So why was Mr. Lawson picking on me?

When Mr. Lawson turned his back to write on the board, Jerry quietly dropped a tissue on my desk. He must have seen me wipe my eyes. Why was everything going wrong?

That night the smell of roast turkey and sweet potatoes drifted up to my room.

"Mark! Deirdre!" my mother called from the bottom of the stairs. "Dinner's ready!"

What was my mother doing home? I went downstairs.

The Christmas tree was trimmed, and the dining room table was set with the fancy china.

"Merry Christmas, Mark!"

"Mom, why are we having Christmas dinner a week early?"

"I'm catering a big party on Christmas day, so we get to celebrate the week *before* Christmas."

"You're just full of surprises," my father said. My mother carried out a platter of sweet potatoes.

"I did all the cooking. What are you complaining about?" She turned to me. "By the way, Mark, when I called home, I had no trouble getting through. I was amazed! Is Duncan's phone out of order?"

"Duncan and I don't talk to each other anymore." I made a dent in my sweet potato and filled it with peas. "We're never going to talk again." I stuffed potatoes and peas in my mouth.

"Mark said Duncan was a nerd," Deirdre said. "That stands for Never-Ending Radical Dude."

"Shut up, zero brain," I said.

My mother looked at my father, and then back at me. My father frowned and started to carve a slice of turkey with the long silver knife.

"White meat, anyone?" he asked. He started heaping Deirdre's plate with food.

Two days before Christmas Mr. Lawson handed out our report cards. I didn't even have to look at mine to know the bad news. I stuffed it into my pocket and walked home alone.

Later I sat in my room and flipped slowly through the pages of my baseball card album. Finally I heard my father call Deirdre and me for dinner.

I went into the dining room and had to smile at how my father had already tried to make the table look Christmasy. There were green paper napkins, green plastic forks, and a glass pitcher of red punch. In the center of the table was a small chicken, roasted to a crisp. He must have been practicing for Christmas dinner.

"Anything new happen in school today?" my father asked. Deirdre and I slid into our seats.

"The fourth grade got their report cards," Deirdre said.

If only Deirdre would evaporate on the spot. Her smile, now minus a few teeth, just grew bigger.

"Can I have a look?" my father asked.

"I don't want to ruin dinner."

"It would be hard to ruin *this* dinner," my father said.

I pulled the folded report card out of my pocket and handed it to my father. He let out a big, disappointed sigh.

"One satisfactory, three unsatisfactories, and math"—he shook his head slowly—"failure. Mark, I was afraid of this."

I poked at the burnt chicken on my plate with the green fork. I didn't know what to say. Even Deirdre kept quiet for once.

My mother burst into the room.

"Merry Christmas, everyone!" She was all dressed up, wearing a black velvet coat and glittery earrings. She smelled like the spice balls we used to make in Ms. Maxwell's class. In her hand was a pan covered with silver foil.

"Let's see, Mom," Deirdre said.

My mother lifted the foil. It was a fruitcake

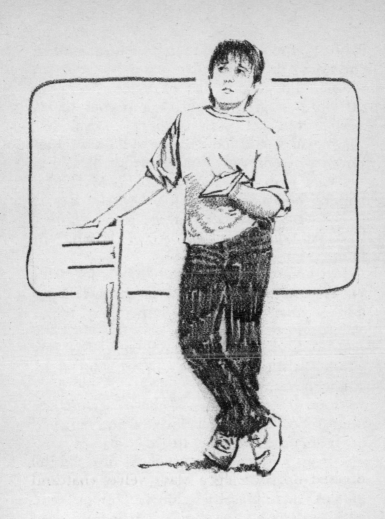

in the shape of a reindeer. It had a candied cherry for the nose.

Something about that cake set my father off. "If you cared as much about your family as you cared about your catering," he exploded, "*this* never would have happened!" My father waved my report card in the air.

"What is it?" my mother asked. My father handed her the report card, and she looked it over. She looked from me to my father. "You're not being fair, Al. This isn't my fault."

"All I know is that Plan A has failed." My father banged his hand on the table. Deirdre looked at me. Then she jumped out of her chair and ran upstairs.

"I think you had better go upstairs too," my mother said to me. I knew better than to argue with her.

Alone in my room, I leaned back on my bed, slipped my baseball glove on, and punched my other hand into it. I heard Deirdre crying next door and my parents' voices rising in the dining room. Then the front door slammed. I didn't know who had left. Maybe both of them. This was going to be some Christmas, I could tell.

A few seconds later there was a knock on my door.

"Yeah?" I didn't care if it was Deirdre. I

really wanted some company. But it turned out to be Mom instead.

"Hi. Can we talk for a minute?"

I shrugged.

She sat at the edge of my bed. She was still wearing the black velvet coat. Her earrings sparkled in the light. But her eyes were red from crying. I reached over to the tissue box beside my bed, pulled a bunch out, and handed them to her. She blew her nose and smiled a little.

"I want to say something about your report card," she said finally.

"Awesome, isn't it?"

"Look, Mark, a bad report card isn't a crime. Why don't you get some help with your school-work? How about Duncan?"

I shook my head. "I told you, I'm never talking to him again."

"Never is a long time. Haven't you two been mad at each other long enough?"

I punched my glove. "How about you and Daddy?"

My mother sighed. "I know. You're right, of course." She frowned. Then she smiled at me. "I'll make you a deal," she said. "I'll swallow my pride and make up with your father. But you have to promise to just try to talk nicely to Duncan too. Is it a deal?"

She waited hopefully. I frowned and turned over on my stomach. "Promise me you'll think about it?" she said.

"Okay." I shrugged. How bad could it be?

Chapter 8

"**D**id you see *Body Parts* in biology last year?" Jerry whispered to me.

"No talking in the halls," Mr. Lawson said. We were walking to the art room. The boys were in one line. The girls were in another.

"It was gross," Jerry continued.

"Shhhh," someone hissed behind me.

"Probably Duncan's body," I said to Jerry in a low voice. We walked silently the rest of the way.

The art room was so cold I could see my breath in little smoke puffs. Mrs. Hearth came into the room with a big wool scarf wrapped around her neck and a sweater underneath her smock.

"It takes a while for the heat to come up

after it's been turned off over the holidays,"
Mrs. Hearth said. She stopped talking for a
second and put her hand to her ear.

"Hear it?" It sounded as if there were ca-
naries in the radiator, the way it did on the
first cold day every year. "Well, I hope you all
had a great vacation and now you're ready to
work with clay. Put on your smocks."

I buttoned up my father's old white shirt
that had a big wine spill on it and a rip under
the arm. I liked wearing it. It came down to
about my knees.

"Mark, Duncan, you can share this clay."
Mrs. Hearth dropped a big wet lump of clay
in the middle of a two-person worktable. Mrs.
Hearth knew we were best friends. But she
obviously didn't know we weren't talking to
each other.

I looked over at Duncan. He looked at me.
I remembered the deal I'd made with Mom.
Maybe I should tell him I was ready to forgive
him for lying. Then I stopped myself. Nope. I
couldn't. I was still mad. Anyway, why didn't
he apologize to me? He'd started it. If he
hadn't hit Mr. Lawson's windshield, none of
this would have happened.

Duncan turned his back on me. "I'd rather
sit with Eric," he said to Mrs. Hearth. Eric?
Duncan wouldn't sit with *me*? But *he* was the
one who was wrong! Mrs. Hearth looked at me.

"Okay," she said. "Sure. Mark, why don't you sit next to Jerry and Scott?"

I felt my face turn red. I couldn't believe Duncan was mad at *me*. I dragged a chair over to Jerry and Scott's table. "Whew! That was a close call." I managed a smile. "I didn't get my cootie shot this morning." Jerry and Scott gave me uncertain smiles.

"I'm going to show you how to make a mug," Mrs. Hearth announced, smiling. She grabbed up some brown clay. "It's really easy, but you have to follow my instructions. Everyone listen." I looked at Mrs. Hearth. This used to be one of my favorite classes. But all I wanted to do now was punch the clay flat as a pancake.

Mr. Lawson agreed to let me go out to the schoolyard after lunch. I ran outside and gulped up the cold January air. Then Jerry, Eric, Scott, Charles, and I wandered over to the baby swings where Deirdre's class hung out.

"Look what I got for Christmas," Jerry said. He spun around in his new red ski parka.

"Cool," Charles said. "I got a boom box, but my mother won't let me bring it to school."

"I got an album for my stickers," Scott said, "and, and . . ."

"And what?" I asked.

"Well, we flew to my grandmother's house

for Christmas Eve, and they served club sandwiches on the plane. I told the stewardess I had a toothpick collection. She let me have all the toothpicks after lunch."

"Ugh, gross!" Eric said, pretending to gag.

"What did you get?" I asked Eric.

"I got video games, but I left 'em all at my cousins'. They're going to mail 'em to me."

"Well, I know what I want for a late Christmas present," I said.

"What?" Jerry asked.

"I want Duncan's math notebook." I looked over at Duncan. He held his notebook tightly.

"Who's going to get it for me?" I puffed up my chest. I felt a push in the small of my back. I turned quickly. It was Deirdre.

"I'm going to tell," Deirdre said to me.

"Mind your own business." I pushed her away. "If you tell, I'll beat you to a pulp." I grabbed her hands and pulled off her new "magic" mittens. They were silver. When it was cold, a picture of a princess appeared on the backs of the mittens. The colder it was, the more of the princess you could see. Now, you could see the whole picture, even the princess's wand.

"Give them back!"

"Maybe, maybe not. That all depends on you." I stuffed them into my pockets. "Now, get lost."

The guys stood around, jumping from one foot to the other to keep warm. Jerry rubbed his hands together.

"It's a little cold to go without gloves," he said, nodding at Deirdre. Deirdre's hands were in the pockets of one of her friends' jackets. The two of them were jumping up and down. When they saw I was looking, they stuck their tongues out at me.

"Come on, enough baby stuff," I said. I looked around at the guys. "Is someone going to get me the notebook or not?"

No one answered. Jerry looked over at Duncan, who was standing by himself near the jungle gym.

"I don't know," Jerry said.

"Doesn't sound like a lot of fun," said Charles.

"Let's build a snowman that looks like Mr. Lawson instead," Scott said.

"You're all just chicken." The ball of anger was growing in my stomach. "Come on!"

Charles shook his head and walked away. Eric followed him. Then Scott.

"See you later," Jerry said.

I watched as they ran to the other side of the playground. I pushed the empty baby swing. It made a creaking, spooky sound. Chills ran up my spine as I turned and walked back

into the school building. What was wrong? Why was everyone acting so strange?

That night I took my usual seat at the dinner table and waited for the usual question from my father: anything new happen at school today? Before I'd get a word in edgewise, Deirdre would tell on me about wanting to steal Duncan's notebook. I waited for the usual. But Deirdre came to the table late, and she carried her baby doll, her baby doll's high chair, and dishes.

My father put a TV dinner covered with foil in front of each of us.

"I see we have a guest tonight." My father nodded at the baby doll. Deirdre smiled. I felt the foil. It was cold in the middle. I peeled it back.

"Dad, I think you're supposed to uncover part of the TV dinner before putting it in the oven," I said.

My father shook his head sadly. "Okay, I admit it, I'm a lousy cook." He uncovered his own dinner and started eating it anyway.

"Baby likes it," Deirdre said, holding a spoonful of frosty mashed potatoes to her doll's mouth.

Dad bit into a cold forkful of roast beef. "Anything new happen at school today?" he asked.

I froze. Here it was. I waited for Deirdre to say something. But she was too busy feeding her doll to notice. "Try some iced peas, they're good for you," she said.

"Mark?" my father said.

"No, Dad, nothing."

Later that night I knocked on Deirdre's door. There was no answer. I peeked in. She was sleeping with her blanket over her head. I could hear her breathing, deep and steady. I tiptoed into the room. The night light made a warm shadow. I could see her doll's head sticking out at the top of the blanket. I put Deirdre's mittens back on her night table. They glittered in the light.

At school the next day Mr. Lawson announced, "We're starting a new unit in social studies." He pointed to the blackboard at the words "Know Your Community."

Underneath he'd made a list of topics: transportation, parks, schools, shopping malls. "We're going to work in committees. Each committee will have a topic and a chairperson. The chairperson will pick three other kids to work with. You'll divide the work and organize the material. No waiting until the last minute to get the work done. And if everyone isn't pulling his or her own weight in the committee, I want to hear about it."

He read aloud the names of the committee chairpeople. I watched people get picked. Eric got picked. Then Scott. Even Duncan. Nobody picked me. I knew it. I looked up at Mr. Lawson. I wanted to die.

"Mark, you can be on Marcie's committee, but any funny business and you'll be on your own committee and responsible for all the work. Is that clear?"

I swallowed. "Yes, Mr. Lawson."

What had happened to all my friends? Duncan lied and I lost my spot on the baseball team. I lost my recess rights, and now I was even losing my buddies. I didn't understand it. And it just wasn't fair.

Chapter 9

*L*uckily for me, it snowed all the way through February, so I had a lot to do around the house. I shoveled the driveway and the path around our house and stacked wood in the yard. I put all my baseball cards in order and oiled my glove until it was as soft as butter. But then the winter thaw came, and my father told me to go outside and play.

I made my way to the baseball field to watch the team tryouts. The ground was so gooey that my sneakers stuck to the mud. I walked to the bleachers and stood behind the fence. The March sun was bright, and I had to put my hand above my eyes to block the glare.

The guys filled the bench behind home plate. Duncan was at the very end of the bench.

Jerry was ready to bat. Mr. Lawson had his eye on him.

Jerry cracked the ball, and it went sailing to center field. Mr. Lawson walked over to Jerry, slapped him on the back, and gave him the thumbs-up sign.

I watched each of the guys go up to bat. Everyone got a turn except Duncan. Then they hopped through the puddles to the outfield for pitching and fielding tryouts. Duncan didn't get up from the bench.

"Hey, Jerry!" I called out. "You in the red!" Jerry looked up. He saw me waving and ran over.

"Hey, Hunter. How's it going?"

"Great."

"Sorry about the team."

"Me too." I shrugged. "Better luck next year, I hope."

The next week I rode my bike past the field during team practice.

"Not underhand!" I could hear Mr. Lawson yell. "Overhand!"

I leaned my bike against the fence and watched. Jerry threw to Eric. The ball went over Eric's head. Then Scott and Charles both ran to catch the ball and bumped into each other. The ball bounced to the ground.

"Get the ball! Get the ball!" Mr. Lawson

yelled in a hoarse voice, hitting his head with his hand.

Out of the corner of my eye I noticed Duncan walking toward me. I turned my back and looked straight at the field. Mr. Lawson was lining up all the guys. He took off his baseball cap and scratched his head. I could hear his voice rising and falling as he walked from one end of the line to the other.

I turned my head quickly and caught Duncan watching me. I frowned and turned my face away.

"Hi," he said.

"Hey," I said back. "How's the baseball going?"

"It's not," Duncan said. "It's not going at all."

I looked back at the field. I could see he was telling the truth this time. Mr. Lawson was still lecturing the guys.

"See ya," I said.

"Yeah, see ya," he said back.

I turned my bike around and rode away.

Duncan had talked to me first. That was kind of like saying he was sorry. That felt good. But I was still mad. I pedaled my bike slowly.

I had a right to be mad. Duncan had thrown the mudball, not me. He got me in trouble.

That wasn't fair, Duncan should apologize to *me* for that.

I remembered the row of mudballs and the wet, gray highway. I heard myself say, "Sink it in there! Now!" to Duncan.

I braked and put both feet on the ground. Wait a minute! Wait one minute! *I* told Duncan to throw the mudball! And I told him *when* to throw it! It was my idea. Mine!

All this time *I'd* been mad at *him*. I never thought he might be mad at me for getting him into trouble. No wonder he'd acted so weird! I rode home as fast as I could.

Back in my room, I sat at my desk and stared at a blank piece of paper. "Dear Duncan," I wrote. I didn't know what to put next. "I'm sorry." I wrote the two words. They looked small and stupid on the paper. I crumpled it up and and pitched it into the wastebasket.

Through the wall I could hear Deirdre playing my worn and scratchy copy of "Here Comes Peter Cottontail." A moment later she appeared in my doorway. She had on a headband with cardboard rabbit ears taped to it.

"Can I borrow your old Dr. Dentons?" she asked.

"Why?" I pictured my old pajamas with the feet and drop seat. They used to be my favorites.

"I'm playing the Easter Bunny in our class play."

"Use your own."

"They're pink. I need yellow. I'm going to hop down the aisle of the auditorium," she said.

I looked at her. I didn't even care about the Dr. Dentons. I got up from my desk and pulled open my bottom dresser drawer. I found the pajamas all the way in the back. "Here," I said. I tossed them to her.

"Thanks, Mark." She caught them and raced out of my room. I stared after her. Nobody had said thanks to me in a long time.

I went back to my desk. I stared at the blank paper. I scratched my head and tapped my pencil. Then I picked up the phone and dialed Jerry's number.

"Hey, dude," I said into the phone.

"Hi, Mark. Did you do the math yet?"

"No. Listen. I just thought of something. You know that mudball? The one that caused so much trouble? I was thinking, Duncan threw that mudball, but, you know, it wasn't his idea. I told him to. Remember?"

I waited for Jerry to say something, but he didn't. "Hello? You still there?"

"Yeah."

"So what do I do?"

"You could apologize."

"Yeah? All right." I hung up. I felt nervous. I looked around my room. My eyes settled on my Babe Ruth poster. He looked so determined. Go for it, Hunter, I told myself. Just as I reached for the phone, it rang. I grabbed it

"Hello?"

Silence.

"Hello?"

"It's Duncan."

I stood up.

"Hi," I said. "I was just going to call you."

"Why?"

"Well, um," I looked at the poster. "Uhhh . . ."

"What?"

"I got it all wrong. Well, sort of. I've been thinking, Dunc. I got you to throw the mudball. You wouldn't have done it if I hadn't told you to. And if I hadn't said, 'Now,' it wouldn't even have hit Lawson's car. So it was really my fault too."

"Yeah."

"I'm sorry, Dunc."

For a minute, all I heard was Duncan's breathing. Then he said all in a rush, "I should never have told on you. That was nasty. Mr. Lawson ran you through the wringer. I'm going to write him a letter explaining everything. I'll give it to him tomorrow."

"I'll sign it too," I volunteered.

"Yeah? Better wear our catcher's masks."

"Yeah!"

We were both quiet.

"Mark, you still need help with math?"

"Wow, do I!"

Duncan's laugh came over the line. "I thought you'd never ask."

◆ Chapter 10 ◆

Monday morning in the schoolyard, Duncan handed me an envelope. I pulled out the piece of paper inside and quickly read it.

Dear Mr. Lawson,

    Here's what really happened with the mud-ball. Mark was showing me how to pitch. I was aiming for a rock. Well, you know my aim. I threw the mudball and missed. It hit your windshield. I'm sorry I said Mark did it. That wasn't true. Mark is sorry we practiced so near the road because it's dangerous and it hurt your car.

Sincerely,
Duncan Dover

I signed my name next to Duncan's, stuck the letter back into the envelope, and gave it to Duncan. But after all that, Mr. Lawson was absent the whole week. So we didn't even get a chance to give it to him right away.

Duncan and I went to the Saturday season opener together. The stands were packed with kids and parents. We climbed up the bleachers and found two seats. Mr. Lawson stood near home plate. He was sneezing and blowing his nose.

The visiting team sat in the dugout. Our team ran to the field.

The first guy in their lineup started practice swinging.

"They look more like football players than baseball," I said. Then I saw that Duncan was gone. I stood up and looked around. Every seat was taken. I didn't see Duncan anywhere.

Then I looked back at the field. Duncan was talking to Mr. Lawson! He was trying to give him the envelope. Mr. Lawson was waving him away. I couldn't believe it! The crowd started to clap and yell.

"Let's go, let's go!"

Duncan didn't move. Finally Mr. Lawson ripped open the envelope.

"Let's go, let's go!"

Mr. Lawson read the piece of paper and

bent down and said something to Duncan. He called, "Time out!" He made a letter T with his hands. Then Duncan and Mr. Lawson started waving at the stands. Who were they waving at? Duncan yelled something. The crowd picked up what he was saying.

"Mark! Mark! Mark!"

"Who, me?" I stood up and pointed to myself.

Mr. Lawson nodded.

"Yes!" I read his lips. He waved me down to the field.

"Excuse me," I said, pushing past people's shoulders. I stepped from one bench down to the next. I got to the first row, jumped to the ground, and ran over to the dugout.

"Mark!" Mr. Lawson said. "Duncan!" He held up the letter. "I hope both of you realize how dangerous it is to throw mudballs . . ."

The crowd started to clap.

"And . . ."

The crowd stamped its feet and yelled. Mr. Lawson looked quickly over to the bleachers and frowned. "Mark, get in there. We need you in the game."

I looked at Duncan.

"Why not?" Duncan said to me.

I stared up at the stands.

"Mark?" yelled Mr. Lawson.

"Yes?" I said.

Mr. Lawson jabbed his finger toward the field. "Play ball!"

On a Saturday morning not long after that, Duncan and I sat in my room eating popcorn.

"Guess what?" I said. "I've been retired from Deirdre duty. My mom hired a baby sitter."

"Great!"

"And she's teaching my father the secret to frying bacon. It's all part of Plan B."

"So does that mean we can go out and play ball?"

"You bet!"

I opened my desk and pulled out my final report card. "And take a look at this."

Duncan looked it over. "You passed math! You passed everything!"

I nodded. "Thanks to you," I said.

Duncan grinned. "C'mon," he said. "We're wasting time. Let's play ball!"